Let's Make a Rainbow

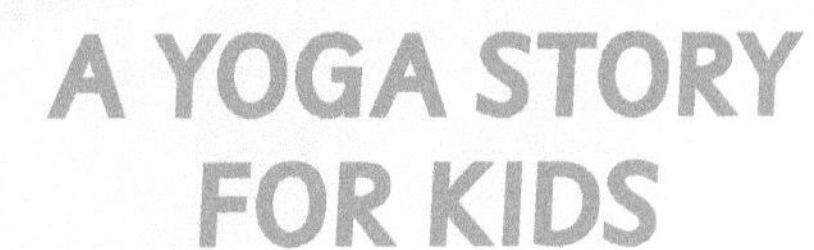

by **SUSAN E. ROSE**
Illustrated by **TIMNA GREEN**

Illustrations by Timna Green
Book design by Travis D. Peterson

ISBN 978-0-578-79563-8 (paperback)
ISBN 978-0-578-79674-1 (e-pub)

For more details about the yoga poses presented in this book,
and a detailed lesson plan for teachers, go to www.susanroseyoga.com

ACKNOWLEDGMENTS

I would like to thank and acknowledge several people who have helped me bring this book to life. Betty Larrea, my mentor and editor, who guided me through this process. Travis Peterson, my book designer who patiently answered so many questions, and Timna Green, for bringing Lily and Lee to life. And most of all to my mother, Bette Rose, for teaching me to believe in myself and giving me Roots and Wings.

DEDICATION

This book is dedicated to all the children I have taught, those who inspired me, and the ones who helped me to become a better teacher. But especially to Kayla and Katie, both of whom I will never forget.

When it's rainy and
there's nothing to play,
use your imagination
to get away.

Lily said to her
little brother Lee,
"Let's do some yoga,
just you and me!"

Yoga makes you happy
when you feel bad,
and can turn the day
sunny instead of sad.

Yoga keeps you calm, and makes you strong.
I love to do it all day long.
Come play with me, learn something new!
Let's discover what we can do.
Yoga teaches you to be kind.
It connects your body to your mind.

I'll be the teacher, just follow me!
What can we pretend to be?
Airplanes, snakes, and volcanoes,
Lions, butterflies and rainbows.
Just watch me, I'll show you how.
Let's play Yoga, ready, set, now!

BUTTERFLY POSE

Feet together, knees out wide, rock yourself from side to side.
Flap your wings like a butterfly. Float your feet up to the sky!
Sit up tall, sit up straight. Lift your heart, you're doing great!

CAT AND COW

On hands and knees, let's make a table, with four steady legs, strong and stable.
Drop your belly, moo like a cow. Round your back and say meow!
Cat and Cow are so fun to do. Moving your spine is good for you!

DOWNWARD DOG

Wag your tail up to the sky, nose down low and bottom up high.
Spread your paws and lift one leg. You can bark but please don't beg!
Now take your Down Dog for a walk to romp and play around the park.

VOLCANO POSE

Jump your feet wide, with your hands at your heart.
Volcano starts rumbling, right from the start.
Inhale with your hands up over your crown.
Hot fiery lava starts to pour down.
Explode in the air, let the sparks fly
out your fingers and up to the sky!

WARRIOR POSE

Warriors are brave, Warriors are strong!
When you stand tall, you can't go wrong.
Flex one knee, sweep your arms out wide.
Don't forget to do the other side!
Warriors are peaceful, Warriors are kind.
They lead with their hearts
and focus their minds.

TREE POSE

Trees give us shade and help us breathe, so spread your roots and grow some leaves.
Stand on one foot, and rise up tall. Keep your eyes steady so you won't fall.
Extend your branches, sway with the breeze. Become your favorite kind of tree!

AIRPLANE POSE

Start your engine, going strong.
Stretch one leg back, straight and long.
Lift your arms and start to fly,
like an eagle in the sky.
Soar in the clouds and look around,
then land safely on the ground.

SNAKE POSE

Lie on your belly, skinny and long, like a snake in the grass, slither along.
Raise up your head and arch your back. Stick out your tongue, ready to attack!
Look around for something to eat. Dining on bugs is such a treat!

LION POSE

Sit on your heels, claws on your knees.
King of the Jungle is resting with ease.
Ready to growl, breathe in through your snout.
Puff up your chest and stick your tongue out.
Let loose a great thunderous roar
like you've never ever roared before!

SLIDE POSE

At the playground, let's make a slide.
Up you'll climb, then down you'll glide.
Sit on your bottom, legs out long,
hands by your hips, arms feeling strong.
Raise your belly up to the skies.
Slide Pose is good exercise!

CHILD'S POSE

When you need to feel peaceful, safe and sound,
find a quiet place, down on the ground.
Head to the earth, sit back on your feet.
Curl up in a ball, feel your heart beat.
Reach for your heels, then breathe nice and slow.
Rest and relax, and let it all go.

Outside the day
is cloudy and gray.
We wish the rain
would go away.
Maybe if we
quit complaining,
we could help it
to stop raining!
We think we know
what must be done.
Salutations to the Sun!

Raise
your
hands
high,
stretch
up
tall.

Then hang down low like a ragdoll.

Feet jump way back, a plank you'll make.

Drop to your belly, hiss like a snake.

Down Dog is next, wag your tail high.

One foot steps up,
arms
reach
for
the
sky.

Roar like a dragon,
breathe fire through your nose.

Feet step together
and tickle your toes.

Stretch
up
tall
and
wave
at
the
sun.

Hands
to your heart,
now you
are done.

RAINBOW POSE

The rain has stopped, and what do you know?
The sun is shining, we see a rainbow!
Let's scoop up the paint and spread it wide.
Paint all the colors from side to side.
A beautiful arc in the sky of blue,
gleaming down from above on me and you!

When you feel blue on a stormy day,
Yoga can make the rain go away.
Salutations will bring out the sun,
a sign in the sky when you are done.
All the colors presenting a show,
so when it rains, make a rainbow!

DID YOU KNOW?

- The colors of the rainbow are red, orange, yellow, green, blue, indigo, and violet. Remember ROY G BIV!
- Rainbows are really a full circle, but we can only see part of it from the Earth.
- Rainbows are created when light shines through water. That's why you see a rainbow when the sun comes out after it rains!
- Rainbows can exist in mist, fog, sea spray, waterfalls and dew.
- Rainbows are often seen as a symbol of hope and optimism.

CPSIA information can be obtained
at www.ICGtesting.com
Printed in the USA
LVHW072345030721
691851LV00002B/7